William Collins Sons & Co Ltd
London · Glasgow · Sydney · Auckland
Toronto · Johannesburg

First published by William Collins Sons & Co Ltd 1989
© Copyright text Colin and Jacqui Hawkins 1989
© Copyright illustrations Colin Hawkins 1989

A CIP catalogue record for this book is available from the British Library

ISBN 0 00 184239 0

Printed in Great Britain by William Collins Sons and Co Ltd., Glasgow

Crocodile Creek

The Crockers on Holiday

Colin and Jacqui Hawkins

COLLINS

It was a bright, sunny morning in Crocodile Creek.
"Ting a ling, ting a ling," went Postman Croc's
bicycle bell.

"Hello, kids," said Postman Croc.

He handed Charlie and Clarrie Crocker a big airmail letter.

"It's from Uncle Ken in Australia," said Dad.

"He's invited us for a holiday!"

"Yippee!" everyone shouted.

The next day the Crocker family set off for Australia
in their houseboat.
They waved goodbye to their friends in Crocodile Creek
and sailed down the river towards the open seas.

On the way the Crockers stopped off in France. They visited the Eiffel Tower and ate lots of French bread.

"Mmm, très bon!" said Dad.

They they sailed on to Spain, where Mum did some Spanish dancing.

In Italy the family ate mounds of spaghetti and lots of delicious ice cream.

Their next stop was Egypt, where they had a ride on a camel.

"It's a bit lumpy!" said Dad.

The camel was very cross.

In India the Crockers went for an elephant ride and ate lots of curry.

Then on they sailed across the ocean.
"Eek, sharks!" cried Clarrie.
But Dad and Gran soon sorted them
out and it was all plain sailing after that.

They sailed on for many weeks, until at last one
morning, Charlie shouted, "Land ahoy!"

There before them was Australia! Soon they were
cruising up a wide, muddy river.

The houseboat chugged round a bend and they had
arrived at Krocker Creek!

"Yippee, we're here!" they shouted.

"Glad to see you, mates!" shouted Uncle Ken as the houseboat reached the bank.

Everyone cheered and there was much hugging, kissing and happy snapping!

The days of the holiday went by very happily. Dad Crocker and Uncle Ken laughed about old times and spent their days eating, drinking and fishing.

Mum Crocker, Auntie Katie and Gran had lots of fun gossiping, shopping and spending time in the beauty parlour.

The young Crockers had a wonderful time. Every day they swam in the creek and played hide and seek with the kangaroos or kiss chase with the sheep.

One day Uncle Ken organised a cricket match.
Another time they had a picnic on the beach.
"Just look at those waves!" cried Gran and shot off to
try her claws at surfing!

One morning the sheep shearers arrived. They came to the farm each year to clip the wool off the sheep.

Dad had a go at shearing but he wasn't very good.
"Bbbah!" said the sheep.

Some of the sheep put on woolly jumpers so they
wouldn't catch cold.

The days grew hotter and hotter. One afternoon it was so hot Mum Crocker went off to the edge of the creek for a paddle.

"Aah, that's better," she said. The cool water tickled her claws and she sat down to relax for a while.

Whoosh! Suddenly a long, black shape swished through the water. It jabbed hard at Mum's leg.

"Eeek! I've been bitten!" she screamed, and she ran for help.

"Something horrible bit me!" she cried.

"Oooh," said Dad and he fainted.

Auntie Katie rushed to the radio and called for help.

"Emergency! Emergency! Come in Flying Doc Croc. Mrs Crocker is really crook! She's been bitten by a snake."

"OK, Katie, I'm on my way," said Doc Croc.

Soon Doc Croc's plane landed at Krocker Creek.
"Let's take a dekko at this snake bite," said Doc Croc.
"Mmm," he peered closely at Mum Crocker's leg.
"Mmm, no swelling there, Ma. Can you show me where the snake was?"

Everyone rushed down to the edge of the creek.
"It was just there," said Mum, pointing into the
water.

"Eeek, it's still there!" yelled Charlie, making everybody jump.

Under the water was a long, dark shape.

"Leave this to me, folks!" said Doc Croc.

SPLASH! He leapt into the water.

There was a lot of splashing and thrashing as Doc Croc struggled and fought.

"Gotcha!" spluttered the Doc and he lifted the snake out of the water. "This is the very deadly-mistake snake," grinned Doc Croc waving a branch in the air.

"So it wasn't a snake after all!" said Mum as Doc
bandaged her foot.
"No, but it had a nasty bite!" said Doc Croc.
They all laughed and Mum felt much better.

Auntie Katie thought they should celebrate with a barb-e-que.

"Now that's a good idea," laughed Uncle Ken, "I could do with a bite!"

So they guzzled and gobbled until they could eat no more. Then it was time for Doc Croc to go.

"Take care, folks!" shouted the Doc, "Watch out for those snakes now!"

They all laughed and waved as the Flying Doc Croc's plane flew off into the sunset.

The Crockers had a wonderful holiday in Krocker Creek, but all too soon it was time to go home.

"Come back again," cried Uncle Ken and Auntie Katie.

"Yeah, come bbback again," bleated all the sheep.

"Come and see us next year," called Mum Crocker.

The houseboat floated further and further away from the riverbank.

"G'day," said Baby Crocker, and they all laughed.